# Where Are My Slippers?
## A Book of Colors

by
**Dr. Carolan**

**illustrated by**
**Joanna F. Carolan**

Kauai, Hawaii

For Sam and Saraya

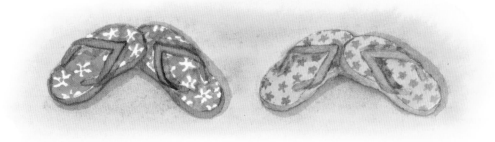

Banana Patch Press
www.bananapatchpress.com

Library of Congress Control Number: 2007903333
ISBN-10: 0-9715333-7-7
ISBN-13: 978-0-9715333-7-0

Printed in Hong Kong

# ZOO ENTRANCE

I lost my slippers at the zoo,
My favorite slippers, which are blue.

I went to the Lost and Found.
They said I should look around.
I looked left and I looked right,
My blue slippers were not in sight.

# Pink

I looked high and I looked low.
I asked a pink flamingo.
The flamingo took a sip of her drink,
And said, "Flamingos only wear pink."

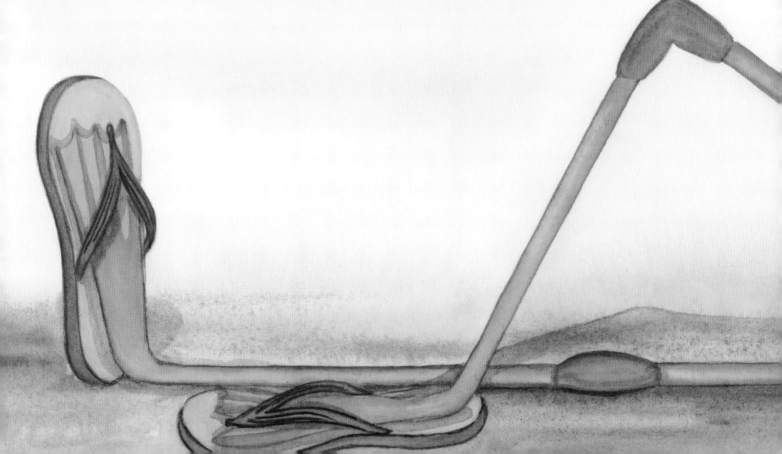

I asked a green iguana next.
He looked at me very perplexed.
He said, " I don't think I have ever seen,
An iguana in anything but green."

Green

# Gray

A gray elephant rested under a tree.
I asked her if she could help me.
She didn't move from where she lay,
But pointed out her slippers were gray.

Yellow

Next I asked a yellow frog
Climbing up an old tree log.
Mr. Frog was a very nice fellow,
But all of his slippers were yellow.

# Black

Then I asked a big black bear,
"Have you seen blue slippers anywhere?"
He was busy eating a snack,
And I could see his slippers were black.

# Purple

A giraffe was wearing a purple lei.
I looked up and called out, "Hey!"
About my slippers, she didn't know,
And her purple slippers each had a bow.

# Red

I figured it couldn't hurt,
To ask a lion in a red aloha shirt.
The lion growled at me and said,
"Can't you see my slippers are red?"

# Brown

A brown kangaroo hopped by.
I thought I would give her a try.
But her slippers were big and brown,
If they were mine, I'd look like a clown!

# Orange

FRESH!
ORANGES

The orangutan was taking a nap,
Wearing an orange baseball cap.
His orange slippers were easy to see,
So I tip-toed away very quietly.

I asked a white pelican flying up high,
"Seen any blue slippers from the sky?"
She flapped her wings and in mid-flight,
Showed me that her slippers were white.

White

Where, oh where could my slippers be?
I wondered, as I gazed out to sea.
I saw blue water and blue flippers,
A blue ball, a blue pail...
But no blue slippers!

At last, I saw at the water's edge,
My blue slippers by a ledge!
Pinned to my slippers was a note.
And this is what someone wrote:

The sand was very hot.
So I borrowed
your slippers.
Thanks a lot!

# Let's say
# The Colors in Hawaiian!

Red — ʻUlaʻula

Yellow — Melemele

Purple — Poni

Blue — Polū

Black — ʻEleʻele

Pink — ʻĀkala

Orange — ʻAlani

White — Keʻokeʻo

Gray — ʻĀhinahina

Green — ʻŌmaʻomaʻo

Brown — Mākuʻe

# Nā Waihoʻoluʻu
## *(The Colors)*

ʻUlaʻula, melemele, poni, polū, ʻeleʻele,
ʻĀkala, ʻalani, keʻokeʻo, ʻāhinahina, ʻōmaʻomaʻo.

My favorite color is bright red, but some days I like purple instead.
I like every shade of blue. And I like pink and yellow, too!

ʻUlaʻula, melemele, poni, polū, ʻeleʻele,
ʻĀkala, ʻalani, keʻokeʻo, ʻāhinahina, ʻōmaʻomaʻo.

Hawaiʻi has many shades of green, most beautiful greens I've ever seen.
The gray clouds come, wind will blow, but then we get a big rainbow!

ʻUlaʻula, melemele, poni, polū, ʻeleʻele,
ʻĀkala, ʻalani, keʻokeʻo, ʻāhinahina, ʻōmaʻomaʻo.

A rainbow's such a colorful thing, it makes me want to shout and sing!
Red and yellow, green and blue, orange and purple are in it too.

ʻUlaʻula, melemele, poni, polū, ʻeleʻele,
ʻĀkala, ʻalani, keʻokeʻo, ʻāhinahina, ʻōmaʻomaʻo.

Learning colors is lots of fun. Melemele is the color of the sun.
ʻEleʻele is the sky at night, moon and stars, keʻokeʻo — that's white!

ʻUlaʻula, melemele, poni, polū, ʻeleʻele,
ʻĀkala, ʻalani, keʻokeʻo, ʻāhinahina, ʻōmaʻomaʻo.

Hawaiian Lyrics: Edith Kanakaʻole
*Reprinted with permission from the Edith Kanakaʻole Foundation*
English Lyrics: Dr. Carolan
Tune: *Little Brown Jug* (folksong)

Guitar & Vocals: Keliʻi Kānealiʻi
Vocals: Brittany Garces, Levi Kānealiʻi, Tia Lardizabal,
Anuhea Panui, Kehau Relacion, Catherine Taylan

*In the Recording Studio, Kaua'i, Hawai'i*
*Back Row (L to R):* Brittany Garces, Anuhea Panui, Kehau Relacion,
Dr. Carolan, John Gilleran, Joanna Carolan
*Front Row (L to R):* Catherine Taylan, Tia Lardizabal,
Levi Kāneali'i, Keli'i Kāneali'i

## About the READ ALONG CD:
Read by: Keli'i Kāneali'i
Guitar & 'Ukulele: Kirby Keough

Executive Producer: Banana Patch Press
Music and Sound Design Produced by Michael Ruff
Recorded, Mixed and Mastered by Michael Ruff on Kaua'i, Hawai'i
*Nā Waiho'olu'u* Produced by John Gilleran & Michael Ruff

KELI'I KĀNEALI'I began singing at the age of four with his church choir.
Born and raised on Oahu, Kāneali'i is the youngest of 15 children. In 1983 he formed
the group *HAPA*. His sultry voice contributed to the international success of the duo.
Since 2001 Kāneali'i has toured the world solo, sharing his contemporary ballads and
traditional Hawaiian songs. For more information email: healaniy@hawaiiantel.net

KIRBY KEOUGH (not pictured) has been playing guitar & 'ukulele since his
"small kid" days. He was born on Oahu. His mother is Hawaiian and his father is Irish-
Norwegian. He has lived on Kaua'i for 30 years where he is a well-known entertainer.
For more information email: keoughk001@hawaii.rr.com

**DR. CAROLAN** was born in Melbourne, Australia. He is a pediatrician in private practice on the island of Kaua'i, Hawai'i. He is married to Joanna F. Carolan.

**JOANNA F. CAROLAN** was born in San Francisco, California. She is an artist and owner of Banana Patch Studio, an art studio and gallery on Kaua'i.

Other Dr. Carolan books available from Banana Patch Press:

*Ten Days in Hawaii, A Counting Book*
*B is for Beach, An Alphabet Book*
*Goodnight Hawaiian Moon*
*Old Makana Had A Taro Farm*
*This Is My Piko*
*A President from Hawai'i*
*The Magic 'Ukulele*

Dr. Carolan and Joanna Carolan would like to thank:

Keli'i Kaneali'i, Kirby Keough, Choir Director Mary Lardizabal, Levi Kaneali'i, Tia Lardizabal, and The Kapa'a Middle School Choir Members: Brittany Garces, Anuhea Panui, Kehau Relacion & Catherine Taylan for their beautiful music

Michael Ruff and John Gilleran for their sound and music production

Healani Youn & Malia 'A. K. Rogers for help with the Hawaiian text

The Edith Kanaka'ole Foundation

Donn and Nancy Forbes

All the keiki in Dr. Carolan's practice

Dr. Carolan's staff: Lisa, June, Laura and Ku'ulei

Dr. Carolan's sons: Sean, Seumas, Brendan and Eamonn

The Banana Patch team: Sheri, Dennis, Jana, Vicki, Naomi, Mitzi, Angela, Brooks, Shanelle, Erin, Michelle, Yoshiko, Patty, Liselle, Crystal, Anna, Patricia, Melissa, Alice and Diana

Tom Niblick of Printmaker in Lihu'e, Kaua'i.

For more information visit:
www.bananapatchpress.com
www.bananapatchstudio.com